Quincy the Quail and the Mysterious Egg

By Barbara Renner

Illustrated by Amanda M. Wells

Life is full of surprises - Enjoy!

Barbara Renner

Copyright © 2019 Barbara Renner
ISBN: 978-0-9990586-2-6
Library of Congress Control Number: 2018968039

Quincy the Quail and his mate, Quella, admire their new home.

"I can't wait for our eggs to hatch." Quella sits on the grassy nest.

"Hoo-hoo, hoo, hoo."

Quella shakes. "What's that sound? It scares me."

Use a QR Code Reader App to hear the Great Horned Owl hoot.

Interesting Fact: The number of eggs a quail lays is called a clutch. The average clutch size is 10 - 12 eggs.

"It's an owl. Let's sit still. Maybe he'll fly away."
Quincy snuggles close to Quella.

Quella shudders. "I don't like owls. They have
big claws. They might hurt our babies."

Quincy stands tall. "Don't worry, I'll protect you
and our family."

Interesting Fact: Great Horned Owls are named for
the tufts of feathers that grow on top of their heads.

All of a sudden ... PLUNK!

A large egg falls next to their home.

"What should we do with it?" Quella hugs her own eggs.

Quincy puffs up his chest. "I'll move it away from our nest."

Interesting Fact: If something happens to the female quail, the male quail will finish incubating the eggs.

Quincy pushes the egg. It does not move.

Quincy shoves the egg. It does not budge.

Quincy jostles the egg. It does not shift.

He climbs on top of the egg. It quivers, and Quincy tips over backward on the other side.

He pops up and blows the topknot out of his eyes. "Whoa! That didn't work."

Interesting Fact: The topknot of the Gambel's Quail is longer than other quail species and is composed of small feathers that are bunched together.

Quincy sits down to think. "Quella, what would you do if one of our eggs rolled away from our nest?"

Quella responds, "I would cry."

"We must keep this egg warm and help the baby hatch." Quincy covers it with his wing.

Quincy and Quella take turns sitting on the six small eggs and wrapping their wings around the one big egg.

Then one day, Quincy and Quella hear "CHEEP, CHEEP, CHEEP."

The chicks cut holes in the shells and up pop their heads. All the eggs hatch, except one.

The big mysterious egg lies still.

Use a QR Code Reader App to hear the Gambel's Quail call.

Interesting Fact: Just before the chicks hatch, they cheep to each other from inside the eggs.

Several days later, Quincy places his head against the large shell.

It starts to vibrate.

It trembles and shivers.

CRACK! SNAP!

Out pokes a ball of fur with a pointed beak.

Interesting Fact: Quail chicks eat beetles, small worms, moth caterpillars, and grasshoppers for the first few days after hatching.

"It's a baby owl!" Quincy shouts.

"Hoo-hoo, hoo, hoo."

Quella looks up. "What's that sound?"

An Owl and his mate sit in the saguaro cactus.
"Don't be afraid. Mrs. Owl and I thank you for
taking care of our egg. I hope we can return the
favor someday."

Interesting Fact: The Palo Verde and Mesquite trees in
Arizona's Sonoran Desert act as nursery plants to the
saguaro cacti. Their leafy branches protect the cacti's
seeds that fall and germinate. The saguaro grows and
outlives its nursery plants by more than 100 years.

RESOURCES

The Cornell Lab of Ornithology, All About Birds
Gambel's Quail
Website, December 18, 2018
https://www.allaboutbirds.org/guide/Gambels_
Quail/lifehistory

The Cornell Lab of Ornithology, All About Birds
Great Horned Owl
Website, December 18, 2018
https://www.allaboutbirds.org/guide/Great_
Horned_Owl/lifehistory

Gambel's Quail Call
The Macaulay Library at the
Cornell Lab Of Ornithology
William W. H. Gunn
November 2, 1978

Great Horned Owl Hoot Recording
Recording copyright Lang Elliott,
Music of Nature
langelliott.com

Nature's Web Of Life, The Soul And Science Of An Interdependent Nature
The Ironwood And The Cactus
Posted by William Graham on November 16, 2011 in *Natures Connections, Natures Patterns*
Website, December 18, 2018
http://www.freshvista.com/2011/patterns-in-naturethe-ironwood-and-the-cactus/

Brian Renner
Brian Renner Consulting
www.brianrenner.com

CPSIA information can be obtained
at www.ICGtesting.com
Printed in the USA
LVHW020806120119
603647LV00002B/2/P